MW00966431

A Christmas to Remember

A Christmas to Remember

ANDY BARTNOWAK

Archway Publishing books may be ordered through booksellers or by contacting:

Archway Publishing
1663 Liberty Drive
Bloomington, IN 47403
www.archwaypublishing.com
1 (888) 242-5904

ISBN: 978-1-4808-1951-1 (sc)
ISBN: 978-1-4808-1952-8 (e)

Library of Congress Control Number: 2015944119

Print information available on the last page.

Archway Publishing rev. date: 09/23/2016

"No Santa Claus! Thank God! He lives and lives forever. A thousand years from now, Virginia, nay 10 times 10,000 years from now, he will continue to make glad the heart of childhood".

Reprinted from **Yes, Virginia, There is a Santa Claus**

By Francis P. Church, first published in *The New York Sun* on September 21, 1897.

❦ Contents ❦

Keep your eyes open, keep your heart open,
and you'll find the magic of Christmas.

—MICHAEL RYAN

1

Doubting Danny

As a young boy, Christmas was by far my favorite time of the year. There was nothing that could beat the holiday season: the glow of the lights hung on the tree, the smell of sugar cookies being freshly baked in our kitchen, the houses on our street all decorated, and of course the excitement to discover what Santa left under our tree when we awoke on Christmas morning.

Growing up, it never occurred to me to question Santa Claus. Like most children, I believed in the magic of Christmas and Santa. I had heard rumors and whispers at school that he was a myth, that it was just something parents made up, but I never really paid any attention to it. There was even an incident where one of my classmates at school told a few of us that Santa wasn't real. When I yelled at him and told him he was wrong, he merely laughed, like he knew something I didn't. He said, "Really, Danny, you still believe in Santa Claus?"

Perhaps it was a combination of that episode and turning eleven that began to shake my faith in Santa Claus. I suddenly started having serious doubts. Maybe Santa wasn't real; maybe it was only something for "little kids" to believe in. I almost let these doubts and fears turn me from a kid who couldn't wait until Christmas arrived to someone who couldn't wait until it was over. It wasn't that I didn't want to believe—I did— but like many kids my age, I wanted and needed proof.

Fortunately, I soon discovered the answers to all of my questions, but it took one very special Christmas for me to find out the truth about Santa Claus.

2

Chief Christmas

I grew up in a small town in the Midwest. My two brothers, Benjamin and Patrick, were like most other younger brothers. One minute, we were the best of friends, and the next, we would argue about something that usually led to an all-out wrestling match between the three of us. That's how it goes with little brothers: you love 'em to death, but they can make you crazy sometimes.

When our arguments did get out of hand, my father would step in and settle things very quickly. He rarely yelled; he would simply look all three of us in the eye with a gaze that went right through us and say, "Danny, Benjamin, and Patrick Ryan, I spend all day dealing with people who can't resolve things in a decent manner. I will not have the three of you acting the same way in my house. Do I make myself clear?" Whenever Dad finished with those five words, we all knew that was the end of whatever dispute we'd had for the day.

Our dad was also our town's police chief. So naturally, when he spoke to us that way, we knew it was time to do as he asked, and quickly!

Having a dad as the chief of police was sort of like having Santa Claus in our house year round because he always seemed to know what we were up to. Every summer, despite Mom's repeated warnings about not going swimming in the creek near our house, we just couldn't stay away. Once we managed our way down there, we always checked to see that no one was around. As soon as the coast was clear, we were jumping into the water and having a great time. It was always a lot of fun until Dad came home from work and announced, "I thought Mom told you guys not to go swimming in that creek!" We could never figure out how he knew we were down there swimming, but somehow he did.

We used to joke that Santa had nothing on our dad and probably kept him employed during the Christmas season to help him with the "naughty or nice list." Of course, that's not to say that my mom was a pushover; she wasn't. Mom was a school-teacher, and she was more than capable of dealing with three boys who seemed to have an endless amount of energy. Our parents were extremely loving and fair with us where our behavior was concerned. There were plenty of times when we pushed the limits of their patience, but they always seemed to know how to handle the situation correctly, even if we didn't realize it at the time.

Christmas was the favorite time of year for everyone in our family. My mom started baking and doing her shopping, and my dad would go into his decorating frenzy about two weeks before Thanksgiving. He would go up to the attic, bring down several boxes of decorations, and make sure all the lights were in working order. He would me-ticulously calculate how many strings of lights were needed for a particular tree or wherever he was planning on hanging them.

Dad never thought decorating our house for the holidays as a chore; it was just something he loved to do. I think he simply wanted to make it special for our family, and looking back on it, he did! Mom used to joke that during the Christmas season, she actually had four kids in the house. Dad would always laugh when Mom said that.

Everyone in our family—and in our town— knew how much my dad loved that time of year. It was the main reason he got his unofficial nickname. Around our town, people often referred to him as "Chief Christmas." The police station was always decorated and had carols playing inside. He always participated in the town's annual Christmas parade. In fact, anything that had to do with the holiday season also seemed to involve my dad.

And of course, there was the famous Ryan Christmas Tree Farm.

3

The Tree Farm

My parents owned a Christmas tree farm about ten miles from our house on the edge of town. It was nestled on sixty acres of rolling hills and long stretches of flat land that seemed to go on forever. After ten minutes of walking in any direction, you were lost in a maze of green pine trees that dotted the snow-covered landscape.

Dad bought the land several years before my parents got married, and he began planting various types of Christmas trees. What started out as a hobby bloomed into a family business. People came from miles away to cut down their own trees and help make their holiday memories. My brothers and I grew up helping my parents on the farm and could probably tell you more than you want to know about Christmas trees. Looking back, our tree farm was just one of the many things that helped make the season special for our family. It was a lot of fun and really helped keep us in the yuletide spirit.

On weekends, we would spend most of our time at the farm. We sold trees, wreaths, and seasonal decorations. Dad would be there whenever he wasn't at work, talking to the customers and their children. He would always remind the kids to be good, that Santa was watching, and then he would say, "Keep your eyes open, keep your heart open, and you'll find the magic of Christmas." Dad said it so many times that it seemed like we could repeat it before we learned what it really meant. It got to the point that when we were at home and Dad started to say "Keep your eyes," we would stop him and say, "Yes, Dad. We know." Then we would finish the sentence for him.

He would look at us, smile, and say, "Glad to know you guys actually listen to me once in a while."

"Dear," my mom would say, "how could they not listen to you? You've been telling them that since they were babies."

"Well, I only say it because it's true."

We all laughed, but the truth was we had no idea how profound our father's words were—and how much they would play a role in our Christmas that year.

4

The Talk

Ben wasn't exactly sure when he first noticed it, but it seemed it was right after Thanksgiving. The weekends were generally our busiest time at the tree farm, which meant working long hours.

When I didn't seem to have my usual Christmas spirit, it was just a matter of time before one of my brothers noticed it. Little brothers can be like that. They notice things other people miss, and then they bug you to death by asking endless questions about it.

"What's wrong with you?" Ben asked as we shook off the dead needles of another freshly cut tree, baled it up with twine, and loaded it on top of the roof of Mr. Thompson's car.

"Never mind. You're not old enough to understand," I grumbled in reply.

Trying to change the subject, Ben reminded me that we were going into town in two weeks to take our annual family picture with Santa.

"Yeah, well you can go ahead. I'm busy." The last thing I wanted to deal with was getting dressed up to go into town and have our picture taken with some guy who wasn't the real Santa Claus anyway.

"How could you be too busy to see Santa?" Ben asked incredulously. "And how do you know you'll be busy two weeks from now?"

"Well, first of all, he's not the real Santa," I said, hoping it would be the end of the discussion.

"Yeah, I know," Ben said defiantly, "but he's one of Santa's helpers. Santa can't be everywhere, especially at this time of year, so he has helpers to give him a hand."

Ben was quite pleased with his answer and figured I would see his reasoning.

Instead, I concentrated on the task at hand. "I've

got to go help the Andersons cut their tree down. You know every year they get the biggest tree they can find, and they always end up needing help. Stay here and wait on the rest of the customers. I don't have time to talk about Santa." I walked away without saying another word.

Ben just stood there, dumbfounded. He had never heard me say anything like that before, and he couldn't figure out why I wasn't as excited about getting our picture taken with Santa as he and Patrick were.

Later that evening, my parents came upstairs as part of their nightly ritual of tucking Ben and Patrick into bed before saying good night. Of course, I was too old to participate in that anymore, but my brothers still looked forward to it.

Just as Dad was finishing up with Ben, he told Dad about our conversation at the farm. Naturally, he asked Dad what was bothering me.

After he listened to Ben's story, my dad said, "Hmm. I'm not sure, although I have a few ideas. Why don't you let me think about it for a little while? I'll talk to Danny about it, all right?"

"Okay, Dad" Ben said, thinking there was no way I would argue with our dad about Santa.

Dad knew more about Santa than anyone the three of us had ever met. Ben eventually dozed off without a worry in the world, especially where his older brother was concerned. He just knew that somehow, Dad would fix everything.

It was late on Saturday afternoon, and the customers had been coming in at a pretty steady pace. I was helping Jimmy, one of our seasonal employees and a classmate of mine, tidy things up for the next day's customers when I saw Dad's pickup truck pull into the lot.

"Hey, Dad, we're almost done!" I yelled as I walked back to the small pole barn where a customer could buy Christmas wreaths and other holiday decorations—or simply warm up by the roaring fire.

"Danny, I need you to give me a hand before you leave."

"Aw, Dad, I need to get over to Kevin's house. We're gonna go ice skating with a bunch of friends down at the pond!" *Nothing like ruining my plans,* I thought.

"Danny," said my dad, giving me that same look that meant we're really not going to discuss this, "this will only take about a half hour. Surely you can help me out for thirty minutes?" The look on my dad's face told me the discussion was over.

I was at least old enough to know that arguing about thirty minutes of work with Dad was futile. Instead, I just sighed and wearily said, "Okay. What do you need me to do?" I at least wanted him to know I was unhappy with this sudden change of plans, but as usual, my dad wouldn't give me the satisfaction of acknowledging my frustration.

"Well, we have to load up about a dozen trees I cut down this morning and load them on the wagon to bring back here. We still have customers who don't want to be bothered with cutting their own trees. They also know I can cut one down that's as nice as any they could find out there. But I don't mind doing it at all. Besides, it's what we do for others that really counts, right?"

"Okay. I guess so. I'll go start up the tractor." I knew he was right about doing for others, but my foul mood from changing my ice skating plans wouldn't allow me to show much enthusiasm in my response.

We had traveled about a half mile in the woods that contained various Fraser fir, Scotch pine, balsam, and spruce trees before we came to a small clearing where the trees were piled up, just waiting to be put onto the wagon. The newly cut trees gave off a fresh aroma of pine. We could smell it in the cold, damp air before we could even see them.

As we loaded the trees, Dad paused for a minute and said, "Danny, I've been meaning to ask you why you told your brother you really didn't want to get your picture taken with Santa this year."

I lowered my eyes to the ground. I knew this question would be coming; I was just hoping it wouldn't be today. "Well," I stammered, "it's not that I won't do it or anything. I just don't feel that excited about it. That's all."

"I see," said my father. "Well, I'm not going to make you if you really don't want to, but I hope you'll do it for your brother's sake. Besides, I have a feeling there's more going on than what you're telling me."

I just stood there and stared. *It's amazing,* I thought. *He can always figure out when I'm not telling him the whole story.* At first, I attributed it to the fact that my dad was a police officer for so long, but I quickly remembered Mom was really good at it as well. *Must be something police officers and teachers learn.* I stayed quiet for a few more seconds, although it seemed like an eternity, before I finally blurted out, "I'm just not sure I believe in Santa anymore." I was relieved to finally tell my father what I had been thinking for months.

"I see," he said in his usual calm voice. "And why do you think that?"

"Well, a lot of my friends say there's no such thing as Santa Claus, and it's just for little kids to believe in. Besides, I've never actually seen him in his sleigh with any reindeer, and I just think I'm too old for that type of stuff anymore."

"Okay. Well, I appreciate your honesty. You know, it's not uncommon for kids to stop believing in Santa Claus as they get older. I think it's up to each person to decide what they believe in."

"You do?" I shot back. I couldn't believe what I

was hearing! My dad, the one person who did everything that involved Christmas, was telling his oldest son it was okay not to believe! It was the last thing I expected my father to say. In fact, if there was any disappointment in my father's expression after what he had just heard me say, I certainly couldn't find it. *Yep, seems like Dad is always full of surprises.*

"I understand your dilemma, Danny, but I want to ask you a question or two."

"Okay," I replied. *What could he possibly ask me?*

"What would you say if I asked if you think Mom and I love you and your brothers?"

"That's easy. Of course you love us."

"But how do you *know* we love you?" countered my dad.

I was almost starting to feel like Dad was treating me like a small child. *What kind of question is that?* "Well," I responded. "You love us because you take care of all of us, you always give us big hugs, and you always tell us that you love us."

"True enough," he replied. "Those are all good examples of how we *show* our love, but can you see love, Danny, or is it something you feel in your heart?"

"Well, I guess I feel it in my heart; it's just something that I know." I still couldn't figure out why my opinion about Santa Claus led to this conversation, but I was pretty proud of my answer. *Come on, Dad. A first grader could have told you that.* Even though I still couldn't see the reason for this discussion, a small voice inside my head kept telling me there was more to this talk than I anticipated.

"Okay," Dad said as he pointed to an empty crate on the wagon. "I want you to take that wooden crate over there and just put in the love you have for your mom and me and place it inside of it."

I looked at him with a bewildered expression on my face. *What is he talking about? That's impossible!* "Dad, how could I possibly do that? You can't take love, put it into a box, and show it to someone. Love isn't something you can see. You know that—everyone knows that."

"So you're telling me that something as strong as love can't be seen? Is that right?"

"Yeah" I replied. "That's exactly what I mean. I

don't understand why you're asking me this. And what does any of this have to do with Santa Claus?"

"You see, Danny, you just helped me prove my point. Love is one of the most powerful emotions that human beings possess. Everyone knows when someone loves them. Even babies can sense the love their parents have for them, even though they can't talk or walk yet. It's not something you can take and put into this crate and show me. I can't even see it, but I know it's there. I know you love us—just as much as we love you. What I'm trying to say, Danny, is that some of the most real things in this world are the ones you can't see. You just know in your heart they exist. You simply have faith and believe, even if you can't see it." He paused for a few seconds to let his words sink in. "Danny, I don't want to decide for you what to believe in or not believe in. I just want you to think about what I said, okay? Just think about it."

I stood there for a minute, trying to figure out what just happened. The last time I felt that way was after I fell on the ice while skating and hit my head. I wasn't hurt, just momentarily dazed. Everything my dad said made perfect sense. In my heart, I knew what he said was absolutely true, yet I couldn't seem to shake my doubts on the subject of Santa Claus. I guess I didn't realize it at the time, but part of my sour mood was that I was starting to let the innocence and simplicity of my childhood years slip away.

As I looked at Benjamin and Patrick, I could see how excited they were for Christmas and how their faces brightened up when we talked about what Santa might bring us on Christmas Eve. *Why don't I feel that same excitement like I used to? Is life really this complicated? Is all this part of growing up, knowing that the guy in the big red suit is nothing more than a myth created to fool little kids?*

"Um, okay, Dad. I will," I managed to say. I finished loading the trees on the wagon, lost in my own thoughts.

Once they were loaded, I jumped up on the wagon as Dad started up the tractor to haul them back to the front lot.

As we drove back through the silent woods

with the snow starting to fall, there was no more conversation between us about Santa. All I could think about was what my father had just said, and I realized I was even more confused than ever.

5

Dad's Idea

At breakfast the next morning, Dad stared out the window at our snow-covered yard. After a few moments of silence he proceeded to tell mom about his conversation with me the previous day. "I had a long talk with Danny yesterday about Santa Claus. He's at that age now where he has doubts about things; it's part of growing up. I told him it's okay if he doesn't want to believe, but I also gave him a few other things to consider. I told him that just because he can't see something doesn't mean it's not real."

"I guess you're right about that," she said. "Danny is just going to have to figure this out for himself.

Are you still going to ask him to help Santa give out gifts this year for the children at the hospital?"

Every year, for as long as anyone could remember, my parents and some of their friends collected presents for the children who were patients at St. Luke's Hospital. One of my dad's friends, Ed McCarthy, would dress up as Santa to deliver the gifts to the kids who were too sick to come home for Christmas. Even though a lot of the children knew it was Mr. McCarthy, they loved when he came to visit.

"Of course I am. Just because Danny is having some doubts right now doesn't mean he can't help out. In fact, you just reminded me of something. Ed hurt himself a few weeks ago jumping off the fire truck while responding to a fire. He sprained his ankle. He'll be fine, but he's still pretty sore. We can't have Santa delivering gifts on crutches, now, can we?" He chuckled. "Do you remember old Sam Cunningham who used to be a mechanic in town years ago?"

"The name sounds familiar, but I don't recall ever meeting him."

"Sam and his wife moved to Lake Holly after he retired. I guess he spends most of his time fixing up old cars. I heard that he and his wife have a few grandchildren now. Anyway, I was going to take a drive out there later today after I get done at the police station."

"Sounds like a great idea. I sure hope he can do it. We certainly can't have the gifts delivered without Santa Claus."

6

Will You Be Santa?

Just like he said, Dad set out in his car to visit Mr. Cunningham that afternoon to ask him to help. The drive took a little longer than usual because there was a steady snow falling. The radio station was playing Bing Crosby's *White Christmas,* and Dad sang right along with the music.

As he neared the Cunningham house and pulled into the driveway, he was greeted by the Cunningham's Labrador retriever. Bear weighed about 120 pounds and had a thunderous bark, but he was one of the gentlest dogs around. Just as Dad finished petting Bear, Sam opened the front door.

"Wow" Dad said, looking at Sam with his beard, which was as white as the snow. "For a minute I thought I was looking at Father Christmas himself."

"Michael Ryan, I mean, Chief Ryan." He laughed. "What you are doing all the way out here? Come inside before you freeze."

"Sam, it's great to see you again. It's been too many years."

Once inside the house, Sam, his wife, and Dad caught up on what they had all been doing for the past few years.

Dad explained how he needed someone to play Santa for the children at St. Luke's.

"I'd love to. It's been a long time since anyone asked me to play Santa, and as you can see, I'm the perfect weight." Sam pointed to his belly. "Consider it done."

"Thanks, Sam. I really appreciate it. Come to my house at about four o'clock on December 23 to pick up Danny, Ben, and Patrick. I'll have my secretary meet you at the police station so you can pick up the presents for the children on your way to the hospital."

"No problem, Michael. I'm always glad to help out."

As Dad said good-bye to Sam, Sara, and Bear, he felt excited and happy when he thought about Sam playing Santa Claus. "Thanks again Sam, this will turn out great. We're really lucky to have someone like you who's willing to help. The kids will really be surprised when they see you. Even without the red suit, you look like Santa!"

As dad got into his car to begin the drive home, he smiled and said in a quiet voice, "this will definitely be a Christmas to remember." Little did Dad know how prophetic his words were, or that the surprises were just beginning.

7

The Visit

On December 23, my brothers and I were just about finished working at the farm. Dad was cutting down a few more trees to take to some families who couldn't afford one. He always tried to make sure that everyone who wanted a tree got one, which was another reason the people in town called him "Chief Christmas."

"Are you two almost done sweeping out the pole barn?" Patrick yelled. "We need to get home and get changed. Mom said we need to hurry up so we can be ready when Mr. Cunningham comes by to pick us up."

Mom yelled, "Come on, boys. We need to get going. I have to get back here to help your father finish up. Let's get moving."

"Okay, Mom. We're coming!" Ben yelled as the three of us raced to her car.

I thought about trying to trip Ben as he ran by me, trying to get to the car first, but with Christmas so close, it was better not to chance it in case Dad was right about Santa.

Our ride home basically consisted of Mom giving us final instructions about how to help Mr. Cunningham deliver the presents. "Remember, boys, as soon as you're done, Mr. Cunningham will drop you off at home. I'll have dinner waiting for you. And one more thing: please make sure to mind your manners around Mr. Cunningham."

"Yes, Mom," we all replied in unison. "We will."

"Where do you think he is?" Ben asked noting that the time was now 4:15. "Mr. Cunningham was supposed to be here to pick us up fifteen minutes ago."

"Probably just late because of the snow," I said. "I'm sure he'll be here soon." I continued to look out the window in silence.

Suddenly, Patrick screamed from the back of the house. "You guys! Come quick. Hurry. You gotta see this. Look!"

What in the world is he yelling about? I wondered. *Probably some new toy he saw on television that he decided to ask Santa for.* I pulled myself away from the window, momentarily forgetting about Mr. Cunningham, and ran to see what Patrick was yelling about.

I stopped dead in my tracks. I could hardly believe my eyes. There was a red sleigh in our backyard. A horse with a set of harness bells was pulling it. In the sleigh, a man in a red suit was waving to us, calling our names, and telling us to come outside.

"Can you believe it?" Ben said. "It's Santa and his sleigh."

Before I could say a word, Patrick put on his coat, hat, and gloves and ran outside.

The Ride

"Santa!" Patrick exclaimed. "What are you doing here? Christmas Eve's not till tomorrow."

Before Santa could respond, Ben flew out the door right behind him and yelled to Santa in an excited voice. He certainly wasn't going to take any chances that the real Santa was in the Ryan backyard without going out to see him. Even though Ben had already written two letters to tell Santa what he wanted for Christmas, he wasn't going to let an opportunity like this go to waste. How often do you actually get to see Santa in your backyard—and in a sleigh no less?

I came out the door last. I had already figured out that "Santa" was Mr. Cunningham. I was a bit surprised at the horse and sleigh though. But I figured, knowing Dad, this was exactly the kind of thing he would do.

"Er, hi, Mr. Cunningham," I said in a somewhat shy voice, remembering what Mom had said about using our manners. "Dad said you would be picking us up in your truck."

"He did, now, did he?" The man in the red suit grinned. "Well, I have to say that I much prefer this mode of travel. It wouldn't look right for me to pull up at the hospital in a truck, would it? And by the way, Danny, why don't you just call me Mr. C?"

"Uh, okay, Mr. Cunningham—I mean Mr. C." *Might as well go along with it,* I thought. Besides, I had to admit that going in a horse-drawn sleigh would be a lot more fun than getting a ride in a pickup truck.

"Okay, boys. Get in. Let's get going, shall we?" asked Mr. C.

The three of us just stood there, not really sure what we should do.

Finally, Patrick piped up and said, "Mr. C, you look just like Santa—and you have a real white beard. You even have a sleigh. Are you the real Santa?"

There was a brief silence that seemed to last forever as I wondered how Mr. Cunningham was going to answer the question.

"Well," he finally said with a slight smile, "it's not important what I think. That's for you to decide."

Ben said, "Dad told us that his friend was going to pick us up in his truck, but you showed up. You sure look like Santa. I think you're either the real Santa or definitely his number one helper, straight from the North Pole."

"Boys," Mr. C said with a twinkle in his eye, "the whole idea tonight is to spread Christmas cheer to some children who could really use it. You can call me Santa or Mr. C—whatever you prefer—but I suggest we get going. There are a lot of children waiting for us to arrive with our presents."

The three of us climbed aboard the sleigh, ready to begin our journey.

"Can I sit in front?" Patrick asked. "I've always wanted to ride in a sleigh."

"Absolutely" Mr. C replied. "Danny, you and Ben get in the back and hang on. We've got several miles to cover before we get to the hospital. And bundle up too; the snow is really starting to come down. All right, Chestnut," Mr. C called to his horse, "let's get going."

The horse immediately responded, and we were on our way.

"Hey, Mr. C!" I yelled over the noise of the ring-ing bells on Chestnut's harness. "Don't forget we have to stop by the police station to pick up the presents first."

"Don't worry about that, Danny. I wouldn't be much of a Santa if I came in a sleigh and didn't have the presents with me already, would I?" He laughed.

And sure enough, in the back of the sleigh, there was a large red bag full of brightly wrapped presents.

I guess Dad must have dropped off the gifts with him earlier. Why did he tell me we were going to pick up the presents at the police station if he already gave them to Mr. C? No sense worrying about it now. We have the presents. I might as well enjoy the ride to the hospital.

As the sleigh made its way through the snow-covered fields, I had to admit I was rather enjoying the ride. Ben and Patrick could barely contain themselves as they continued to ask Mr. C one question after another.

"How come you have a horse and not your reindeer?" asked Patrick.

"Yeah. And how come you're here with us and not back at the North Pole in your workshop, getting ready for your trip?" added Ben.

"Well, first of all." He laughed again. "My reindeer are back in their barn, resting up for my big ride. I think it's important, at this time of the year, to do what we can for others, especially those who really need our help."

"That's true," said Ben. "My mom and dad always say one of the best things we can do is help out those who are unable to help themselves."

"Well," Mr. C said and smiled warmly, "your folks are absolutely right. Giving our time to help others is one of the best gifts we can give." Mr. C continued to drive the sleigh through open fields and forests—as if he had been through them a million times before—all while answering more questions from my brothers.

Finally, I decided to join in on the conversation. "Mr. C, do you know how to get to the hospital?" I was concerned because I didn't recognize exactly where we were going even though I knew the hospital wasn't that far away. And the more I thought about it, the more I wondered why Dad didn't tell me about the sleigh. But then I figured it was exactly the type of thing my dad would do for us, especially at Christmas.

"Don't worry, Danny," Mr. C replied. "I have a pretty good sense of direction."

"Yeah, Danny," Ben said, "I'm pretty sure if he can fly around the world in one night, he can get us to St. Luke's without any problem. Right, Santa?"

Mr. C chuckled. "Your brother's right, Danny. I promise I'll get us there safe and sound."

"Okay, no problem, Mr. C," I replied, mindful of my mother's instructions on being polite. "I didn't mean to doubt you. I'm just sort of lost with all the snow and it being dark and all."

Mr. C turned around quickly, and his expression

let me know he was not offended by my question. "It's okay, Danny. You're at an age where you have lots of questions, but try to have a little more faith. Sometimes you just have to believe." He turned around and continued his conversation with my brothers.

Seems like I've heard that before, I thought. *Dad must have really told Mr. Cunningham all about me.* As I sat there, the thought occurred to me that maybe Mr. C was talking about more than just knowing how to get to St. Luke's Hospital.

The snow was coming down in a heavy blanket, and the visibility wasn't very good, but it didn't seem to bother Mr. C or Chestnut as we continued on our journey.

When we approached a small clearing, Mr. C announced, "Boys, here we are."

And sure enough, there was St. Luke's Hospital. *That's why I didn't recognize anything. We came in the back way!* I didn't know anything about Mr. C other than he was a friend of my father's, but I had to admit, he really knew what he was doing when it came to playing Santa Claus. *My brothers will be talking about the sleigh ride for months.* I laughed to myself.

Mr. C interrupted my thoughts as he stopped the sleigh. "All right, boys. Let's get out and deliver these presents. There's a lot of boys and girls waiting for us to deliver some Christmas magic. Let's get a move on, shall we?"

With that, Mr. C and his three helpers walked around the side of the hospital and into the main lobby entrance, ready to surprise the children at St. Luke's.

9

St. Luke's

Inside the hospital, Dr. Peterson, the head of the children's pediatric unit at St. Luke's exclaimed, "Santa, it's great to see you again. The children are really looking forward to your visit. Boys, I'm glad you're helping out again this year too. This visit does a lot to brighten their spirits. By the way, how was the traffic? It's really coming down outside." He pointed to the parking lot. The cars had several inches of fresh powder on top of them.

"We came in a sleigh," I replied. Before I could give Dr. Peterson the scoop on what had happened, my brothers told him all about our ride. Just as they were finishing their story, we were greeted by other nurses, doctors, and hospital staff, who now realized Santa, was at the hospital.

Shouts of "Hi, Santa! Merry Christmas!" rang out from staff and visitors alike as Santa made his way to the children's ward carrying his pack full of presents.

In the pediatric unit, a thunderous roar of voices yelled, "He's here! He's here!"

Mr. C replied back with a hearty "Ho ho ho" and "Merry Christmas, boys and girls."

The children shrieked with delight. It was quite a scene. A few boys nearly fell over each other while trying to get closer to Mr. C. Three girls near the back of the room nervously clutched their Raggedy Ann dolls so hard the tips of their fingers were white. Yet they and all of the children had big smiles on their faces.

Mr. C spent the next two hours visiting the children and presenting them with special gifts. He even visited the children who were too sick to participate, and he left a gift for each of them.

The three of us also spent time talking to the

children. Ben loved telling them about the sleigh ride to the hospital, and Patrick told them about how Santa had surprised us at our house.

Although I was still skeptical, I had to admit that Mr. Cunningham was the most convincing Santa I had ever seen. *The kids really love him.* As I watched the scene unfold before me from the back of the room, I realized I might have spent too much time looking for proof that Santa existed. *Maybe I'm missing the point altogether. Maybe it doesn't matter whether Mr. C. is the real Santa or not.*

The children at St. Luke's were so excited about his visit and the joy they were experiencing that they didn't need to know all the answers about him. Santa was there—and that was good enough for them.

I guess Dad was right, I thought, remembering the words he had spoken to me earlier.

Mr. C led the children at St. Luke's in a rousing chorus of "Jingle Bells."

At that moment, there was no doubt—no matter what anyone said—Mr. Cunningham was Santa Claus that night.

After all of Mr. C's visits, the four of us made our way back down to the lobby. We said our final good-byes to everyone at the hospital and walked back toward the sleigh.

10

Home

The snow was still falling as Mr. C checked over his sleigh.

Ben and Patrick were feeding Chestnut slices of apples that Mr. C had brought with him and talking in excited tones about how much fun they had.

"Well, boys, I hope you had as much fun as I did. I want to thank the three of you for helping me out tonight. I'm very proud of all of you," Mr. C said.

"It was the best time," said Patrick. "Can we do it again next year?"

"Absolutely," Mr. C said with a smile. "Now hop

in and let's get going. Your folks will be expecting you home soon."

The sleigh began its journey effortlessly as Chestnut heeded Mr. C's commands. Except for the rhythmic ringing of the bells, it was completely silent as we traveled through the forest. I sat in the back and thought about everything, trying to make sense of it all. Even though I didn't fully comprehend what was happening at the time, I felt enormous pride and happiness for the joy we brought to the children at St. Luke's.

As the sleigh continued through the snow-covered fields, Ben and Patrick each got to take a turn driving the sleigh. I even got a turn to take the reins, which I had to admit was one of the coolest experiences in my life. It was certainly a lot more fun than driving a noisy tractor.

As we got closer to our house, Patrick said, "I wish this night didn't have to end, Santa. I had a great time!"

"Yeah. Me too," Ben added. "I knew this would be fun, but I had no idea it would be this exciting."

I couldn't hold back from saying, "I didn't know

what to expect tonight, but I never thought it would turn out like this."

"I hope that means you weren't disappointed, Danny," Mr. C said with a chuckle.

"No, sir. Absolutely not." I reached over and hugged my brothers. "It was the best—just like they said." As the oldest, I wasn't really big on hugging my brothers, but I realized they had helped me recapture some of the Christmas spirit I was afraid I had lost.

"Boys, I could never have pulled this off without your help. Really, it is I who owe you a big thank you—and, of course, a Merry Christmas."

With that Mr. C let out a hearty "Ho ho ho" and even Chestnut seemed to sense the excitement and picked up the pace.

When the sleigh finally made its way to our backyard, Mr. C brought it to a gentle stop and hopped out first. "Well, boys, it's getting late. You have to get inside for dinner. And I've got a long way to go before I get home."

One by one we jumped out of the sleigh and onto the snow-covered yard. Ben and Patrick patted

Chestnut on his nose and thanked him for making it such a smooth ride. They turned around slowly to say good-bye to Mr. C, but it was almost impossible to get the words out.

Sensing their uneasiness, Mr. C said, "You three are the best helpers I could ever hope for. It has been my privilege to work with you tonight. Tell your folks I said hello, and rest assured, I will be back to your house on Christmas Eve—with some surprises for you under the tree on Christmas morning."

Patrick and Ben rushed toward Mr. C, gave him a big hug, and said, "Thanks, Santa, and Merry Christmas to you too."

As I stood there and watched, I found myself getting caught up in the moment. "Thanks, Santa. Merry Christmas," I said somewhat sheepishly.

Mr. C. stood there for a moment and replied softly, "Merry Christmas, Danny. Maybe tonight you got answers to some of those questions that have been bothering you for so long, huh?"

"I believe I did, Santa. I really do," I said with a huge smile.

After our good-byes, we walked toward the back

door while trying to watch Mr. C and his sleigh as it drove away. Even when we couldn't see the sleigh, we could still hear the sleigh bells. Eventually, that sound disappeared too. For a brief second, we all looked at each other.

"Unbelievable," I said as I replayed the events of the past several hours in my mind.

"It sure was." Said Ben who looked like he wanted to go and run after Mr. C's sleigh just so the night wouldn't end.

Suddenly Patrick began running toward the back door, screaming, "Wait till Mom and Dad hear what happened!"

Ben and I ran after him.

As the three of us burst in the door, Mom and Dad were surprised to see us come in from the back door instead of the front. Before they could ask who dropped us off and why didn't they see Mr. Cunningham's truck pull into the driveway, both Patrick and Ben were trying to talk over each other, telling them what had just happened. Of course, this meant that Mom and Dad couldn't hear a thing that made any sense. They continued talking at the same time only to be interrupted by Mom occasionally asking a question like, "What do you mean he brought you in a sleigh?"

Finally, the chaos was more than Dad could take. He let out a loud whistle that stopped us in our tracks.

"Okay, now that I have everyone's attention. We want to hear what happened, but it has to be one at a time. Your mom and I can't make heads or tails of what you're saying when everyone is talking at once."

For the first time since we arrived home, I spoke first. "Everything is okay. We had a great time."

"Sure did," Patrick said.

Ben added a huge laugh.

For the next hour, the three of us told Mom and Dad every detail of our adventure with Mr. C.

Mom and Dad seemed completely surprised by our version of what had happened, asking a number of questions.

"Gotta hand it to Sam," Dad said after the discussion quieted down. "He sure went out of his way tonight for the children at St. Luke's."

"He most certainly did," Mom said as she removed a delicious-smelling pumpkin pie from the oven. "You know what? I baked two pumpkin pies today. We have more than enough for ourselves. Why don't we take one to the Cunninghams tomorrow to thank Sam for doing such a wonderful thing?"

We all agreed it was a great idea, and with that, we made our plans to visit the Cunninghams on Christmas Eve.

11

Christmas Eve

After breakfast, we all went to the farm to attend to any customers who were making last-minute Christmas tree purchases.

After completing the final sale, Dad heard a call come out over his police radio and announced that he had to leave. An unfortunate motorist slid off of the road—no one was hurt—but Dad wanted to wait with him until the tow truck arrived.

Mom and the three of us started to clean out the pole barn, and we began the process of putting things away until next season.

When Dad finally returned, he announced that the whole family would be traveling together in his police car to go visit the Cunninghams.

"Cool," Patrick said with a devilish smile. "Can we put the lights and siren on?"

Ben and I started to laugh.

"I don't think so, guys. It wouldn't look very good with me racing off with my lights and siren on and my whole family in the car, would it?"

"No, but we'd sure get there a lot faster," I replied, which caused Ben and Patrick to start roaring again.

"Okay, you three," said Mom in her "teacher" voice. "Enough silliness for now. We've got to get going. After all, it's Christmas Eve, and we're going to be very busy tonight."

I got to sit in the front with Dad while Mom, and Ben and Patrick sat in the back. On the way, we kept reliving the events of the night before, which started the discussion all over again.

Dad asked what I thought about everything that had happened with Mr. Cunningham.

"Dad, I realize I probably spent too much time

worrying about Santa Claus. Maybe I was missing out on the most important thing."

"What do you mean?" Dad's voice told me he probably knew what I was going to say next.

"Well, last night at the hospital, no one cared who Mr. Cunningham really was. To everyone there, especially the children, he was Santa Claus. He delivered presents and brought so much joy to everyone. I realize now that Santa exists in us whenever we do something for others, and to me, that means Santa is as real as anything else in the world."

Dad paused a second before speaking, first checking his rear view mirror to see that his two younger sons were still engaged in a conversation with Mom. They were not the least bit interested in the discussion he was having with me. "Danny, I'm very proud of you," he said, beaming. "Sometimes the best way to come up with an answer is to find it out for yourself, and that's exactly what you've done. If I had told you the same thing, it probably wouldn't have had the same effect. Better that you figured it out instead. It sounds like you had some Christmas magic last night."

"Dad, you're not gonna tell me to keep my eyes open," I said, but before I could finish Dad's favorite saying, he just turned and laughed.

"No need to, son. You already experienced it firsthand."

When Dad pulled into the driveway, everyone scrambled out. Dad rang the doorbell, and we heard Bear barking. "Well at least the dog is home," my father said.

"Dad, can we go in the backyard to look for Mr. C's sleigh?" Ben asked.

"Yeah, can we, Dad?" Patrick asked. "Maybe we can go for another ride?"

"I never realized he even had a sleigh, much less a horse, but no, you guys stay here. The snow is really starting to come down, and I don't want the three of you wandering off in Sam's yard before he even knows we're here." Dad continued to knock on the door, which only caused Bear to bark even louder.

"Michael," my mom said, "I don't think they're home. Maybe they went out to the store for some last minute groceries. Let's just leave a note. We can stop by and see them after Christmas."

Just as Dad began to walk down the steps to get a piece of paper from his car, a vehicle pulled into the driveway. A woman, in her late sixties by the looks of her, got out of her vehicle and walked toward the front porch. She introduced herself as Mrs. Olsen, a neighbor of Sam and Sara's. She had seen Dad's police car in the driveway and was worried that something was wrong.

"Oh, no. Everything's okay. My name is Michael Ryan. This is my wife Karen and our boys: Danny, Ben, and Patrick. I'm the police chief back in town and a friend of Sam's. We just wanted to drop off this pumpkin pie and say thank you for a favor he did for us."

"Oh, I see," Mrs. Olsen said. "Unfortunately, they're gone. I had to drive them both to the airport early yesterday morning. Their oldest daughter is sick, and they decided to fly out to help her with the children. They won't return until December 29. In fact, I also have to pick them up from the airport when they get back."

For a brief moment, there was complete silence from everyone. We were all thinking the same thing.

Dad said, "Mrs. Olsen, are you saying that Sam and Sara were on an airplane yesterday morning?"

"Yes, that's exactly what I mean," she replied in a confused tone. "Is there a problem?"

Before I could say, "That's impossible," Dad cut me off. He said, "No, there's no problem, but it's just that, well, it's a long story. Sam was supposed to do something for me yesterday."

"Oh, yes. Now I remember," said Mrs. Olsen. "Sam told me all about it on the ride to the airport. He said he had promised to help someone at St. Luke's or something of that nature. I don't remember all the details, but I know he said he left a message to let the person know he wouldn't be able to help. I know he felt bad about it. Was that you he was talking about?"

Dad just stood there motionless, trying to completely grasp what she was saying.

I immediately knew something was wrong. *If it wasn't Mr. C who came to our house last night, then who was it?*

"Um, yes, that would be me," Dad replied. "Sam was going to help us out at St. Luke's, but it's okay.

We got everything taken care of. One more thing, Mrs. Olsen, do you know if Sam owns a horse or a sleigh?"

Mrs. Olsen laughed. "A horse and sleigh? No, not Sam. He has a couple of cars in the barn in the backyard—and the only animal he has ever owned is Bear. Why do you ask?"

"Oh, just curious. Well, anyway, I hope their daughter and her family are doing okay. Please wish them Merry Christmas for us."

"I most certainly will," replied Mrs. Olsen. "It was very nice meeting all of you. Merry Christmas."

"Merry Christmas to you too," we replied.

Just as Mrs. Olsen was getting back into her vehicle, Mom walked over to Dad's police car, retrieved the pumpkin pie, and handed it to Mrs. Olsen. "Here you go," she said. "I hope you enjoy it."

"Why, thank you so much. That's awfully thoughtful of you," said Mrs. Olsen. "Sorry you had to come out here for nothing."

"No problem at all," Mom said with a smile. "And believe me, the trip out here was very worthwhile."

As we watched Mrs. Olsen back out of the

driveway, I had that same strange feeling in the pit of my stomach as I did when I observed Mr. C with the children at St. Luke's. I was beginning to understand what had really happened. Suddenly, it hit me like a bolt of lightning. Mr. C wasn't Mr. Cunningham; Mr. C was actually Santa Claus! I think I realized it after we left the hospital last night, but now I was more certain about it than ever. "Dad, do you know what this means?" I asked in an excited voice. "The *real* Santa Claus came to our house last night."

"Yeah, Dad. Danny's right," Ben said. "She said Mr. Cunningham was at the airport early yesterday morning. There's no way he could have been back to our house by the afternoon."

"Dad," I said, "I just remembered that we never even went to the police station with Mr. C to pick up the presents."

"What do you mean, you never went there." Dad asked. "Then what presents did you hand out?"

"Santa's presents," Patrick said with a huge grin.

"Don't you guys remember?" I turned toward Ben and Patrick. "I asked if he knew how to get to the police station to pick up the gifts. He said he already had them—and that he wouldn't be much of a Santa if he didn't already have the presents with him. And they were in that big red bag in the back of his sleigh."

"Do you mean to say that he never went to the station at all?" said my dad who looked like someone had just hit him in the face with a snowball.

"Yeah," offered Ben. "We went straight from our house to St. Luke's."

Dad walked over to his police car. He started the car and grabbed the radio microphone. "Chief to station," he barked into the radio.

"Station, go ahead. Chief is that you? This is Nancy. Everyone else is out. We have some minor accidents with all the snow, so I'm taking over the radio. Is everything okay?"

The rest of us crowded around to listen to the conversation. We all knew Nancy Baldwin. She had been an assistant to every chief of police for the last thirty years. She had known Dad his whole career—even when he first started out as a young patrolman. Dad always said that Nancy was the one person who could keep him on task with his duties. He often joked that if it weren't for Nancy, he would have left his job a long time ago. It was a compliment to how efficient and organized she was.

"Yeah, Nancy. Everything is fine," he said. "Did anyone call me yesterday and leave a message?"

"Well, you have several messages, but I did take a call from a Mr. Cunningham. He said he was not going to be able to do a favor that he promised because of a family emergency. I left the note on your desk. I thought you would be in later, and then we got so busy, I forgot to call and let you know. Also, those presents for the kids at St. Luke's are still here. I thought someone was coming to get them yesterday. Sorry, Michael. Hope I didn't make things worse."

Dad immediately began to rub his forehead. Whenever Dad did that, it meant he was deep in thought and was a signal for us not to interrupt him with questions. He wanted to tell Mrs. Baldwin what was going on, but it would take too long to explain something like this to his secretary. He wasn't confident she would even believe him. I'm not sure

Dad knew what to believe at that moment. Instead, he said, "No problem, Nancy. Everything worked out just fine. Merry Christmas."

"The same to you, Michael," she said. "Merry Christmas to Karen and the boys as well."

Dad put down the microphone.

All five of us stood in the driveway as the snow fell down upon us.

Patrick and Ben began to yell as loud as they could, "We told you guys it was Santa, but no one believed us!"

"Yeah," Ben added, "remember how he told us we could call him Mr. C? Mr. C wasn't for Mr. Cunningham; it was for Claus. Get it? Mr. C meant Mr. Claus!"

"They're right," I said, "There's no way that was Mr. Cunningham, and no one else knew to come to our house to take us to St. Luke's. It was the real Santa Claus!"

The words "real Santa Claus" were still ringing in Dad's ears as we all got back into his car.

Ben and Patrick were so excited they couldn't stop talking over one another. In the end, it didn't matter; they both knew what the other was saying. As my father began the drive home, he tried to sort out everything that happened, much as I had done the night before.

Mom seemed to sense Dad's thoughts. She leaned over and asked, "Why so quiet, dear?"

"Well, for one, it's hard to get a word in with those two carrying on." He laughed. Then Dad got a serious look on his face and said "but I just can't figure out how all of this happened."

I turned to him and stared. I knew, as did my brothers, that last night we'd had the experience of a lifetime. We got to ride with Santa Claus in his sleigh and deliver presents to children who really needed some Christmas magic. I realized I had found all the answers I was looking for. I had discovered my Christmas spirit again, which was burning as bright and alive as ever inside me. I also knew—once and for all—that Santa exists, no matter what anyone said. (I still believe it to this day!)

Ben and Patrick stopped talking and looked at Dad with bewildered expressions. They couldn't believe what they had just heard him say.

Even Mom had a big smile on her face. It was like she knew a secret. "Really, dear? You—of all people—don't know how this happened? The one person who knows more about Christmas than anyone I know of can't figure this out?"

But before Dad could respond, I looked at him and exclaimed, "Dad, remember? Keep your eyes open, keep your heart open, and you'll find—"

All at one time, four voices said, "The magic of Christmas!"

Dad didn't say a word, and it looked like his eyes were moist. He smiled from ear to ear and said, "You're absolutely right. It was right in front of me, and I didn't even see it. I've been so busy telling everyone else to keep their eyes open—and I forgot to do it myself. I guess you're never too old to learn that, even I need to be reminded once in a while too." He smiled.

"It's okay, Dad," I said. "From the way Santa talked about you last night, you're still gonna be on the *nice* list. Don't worry."

And with that, everyone burst into laughter. The drive home in the snow didn't seem to bother my father at all as he contemplated the miraculous discovery we had all just experienced. We continued to talk about what happened over the last twenty-four hours, and then we decided to sing along to *Santa Claus is Coming to Town,* which Frank Sinatra was belting out on the radio.

It had already been a day filled with surprises for the Ryan family, and Christmas wasn't even there yet. All we could think about was what other Christmas magic might happen when Santa came back to our house later that night.

Author's Note

Thank you for purchasing *A Christmas to Remember*, I hope you enjoyed it. If you would like to order additional copies or provide your rating/review of the book, please visit us at www.andybartnowak.com

For every book purchased on our website, a portion of the proceeds will be donated to the *Jenna Kast Believe in Miracles Foundation*. This non-profit organization was named after Jenna Kast, who lost her battle with brain cancer in 2010. The foundation provides support and gifts to children who are battling life threatening illnesses.

www.believeinmiracles.org

About the Author

Andy Bartnowak has been his family's official expert on Christmas since his early childhood. Even during his twenty-two year career as a Special Agent with the FBI, he's been extensively involved in all things Christmas. Andy lives in Michigan with his wife, Karen, their three sons, and their golden retriever Cooper.

Printed in the United States
By Bookmasters